MW01268641

concept of grace. Nick Twomey tells a vivid
story, right out of his own life, that offers
a powerful and highly memorable picture
of what it means to receive something
we absolutely do not deserve. I love the
raw honesty of this delightful memoir,
and I'm grateful for a simple story that
will linger with me for a long time."

– NANCY BEACH
Teaching pastor and
executive vice president for the arts,
Willow Creek Association

"Laugh...cry...and cheer as Nick lurches
from fear to gratitude and finally to an
understanding of grace. A good read.
Read it with someone you care about."

– MICKY GROOTERS
Retired professor of communications,
Northwestern Michigan College

"WRECKED has the power to
repair a broken life. I loved it."

– DAN WEBSTER
Founder,
Authentic Leadership, Inc.

When life crashes in
on you...and what
to do when it happens

WRECKED

Nick Twomey

MEH
PUBLISHING
Traverse City, MI

Published by MEH Publishing
Traverse City, Michigan

Publisher's Cataloging-in-Publication Data
Twomey, Nick.

    Wrecked : when life crashes in on you / Nick Twomey. – Traverse City, MI : MEH Pub., 2009.

    p. ; cm.

    ISBN: 978-0-9840529-0-5

    1. Traffic accidents—Psychological aspects.
    2. Grief—Reconciliation. 3. Twomey, Nick.
    I. Title.

HE5614.T866 2009
363.125—dc22

Project coordination by Jenkins Group, Inc.
www.BookPublishing.com
Cover design by Stephanie McCrumb
Interior design by Yvonne Fetig Roehler

Printed in the United States of America
13 12 11 10 09 • 5 4 3 2 1

To my father,
James Francis Twomey,
an ordinary man who had an
extraordinary impact on my life.

To my children,
Stephen and Krissie,
whom I love
more than words can express.
I pray I have showed you just a bit
of the love my dad showed me.

"It's what you do, unthinking,
that makes the quick tear apart;
the tear may be forgotten
but the hurt stays in the heart."
– Ella Higginson

"A foolish son brings grief
to his father…"
– Proverbs 17:25

"DOH!!!"
– Homer Simpson

CONTENTS

ACKNOWLEDGMENTS

I am a reluctant writer. Call it laziness, insecurity or something else, but I can find a million excuses to avoid putting my thoughts in writing. Most of the excuses are on ESPN, Fox Sports, or in someone else's book.

But over the years I have had some persistent friends who have encouraged me to put in writing what thus far has only been communicated orally. Among the most persistent has been my lovely bride, Rose, a woman whose beauty surpasses her name. She knows the real me and loves me anyway. I'm still scratching my head over that one.

Four other friends have shown irrational amounts of belief in me. Special thanks to David and Jill Hall and Mike and Krista Bullard – four faithful friends for the long haul. As we've said many times, "We belong in a home!" That day is coming soon enough.

To the talented team at the Jenkins Group (Jerry Jenkins, Leah Nicholson, Yvonne Roehler, and Rebecca Chown), to Stephanie McCrumb who provided graphic support and amazing amounts of kindness, to Mickey Grooters who offered helpful insights to the manuscript, to the superb staff I get to work with every day, and to the faith community called Bay Pointe that allows me to tell stories...thank you all.

CHAPTER ONE

Oreo Cookies

Have you ever said or done something so obviously wrong, so publicly wrong, so embarrassingly wrong that in spite of your instincts to bob and weave and try to shift the blame – to extricate yourself from any wrongdoing – you simply can't?

When I was five years old, I was sent to spend the night with some friends of my parents. I don't remember who they were or why I was sent there. I suspect my parents had to be out of town and we, the eight Twomey children, were parceled out to multiple homes. All I remember is being without my brothers and sisters and feeling scared.

Whoever these people were, they were nice. They did their best to make me feel at home. I remember having a bedroom of my own, which was both odd and exciting. I always shared a bedroom with at least one of my brothers, and sometimes all four of us shared a bedroom. Having a bedroom of my own could only mean one thing: these people were rich!

Their wealth was confirmed at dinner. Not only was there plenty of food – enough for seconds, which was a rarity in our family of ten unless you ate faster than anyone else – but Oreo cookies were brought out for dessert.

Oreos! Store-bought cookies! To my five-year-old mind, Oreos screamed *"Money to spare!"* Never mind that home-made cookies tasted better; Oreos were in a league of their own.

Sometime in the middle of the night, I woke up with one thing on my mind – Oreo cookies. Maybe they were calling out to me in my dreams. All I knew is that I had an obsessive desire for a midnight snack.

Off to the kitchen I went, tiptoeing in my best Ninja stealth mode. I was too short to reach the cookie jar, so as quietly as possible, I brought a chair over to the counter, careful not to drag the legs across the floor and make noise. I climbed up, opened the cookie jar, and jammed an entire cookie into my mouth. My moment of bliss was ruined when the kitchen light suddenly went on.

My heart stopped. There stood Mrs. What's-Her-Name (I literally can't remember her name; I'm still too traumatized). She stood there looking at me, white cream on her face, spongy curlers in her hair. I was sure the butcher knife was behind her back.

Busted, with nowhere to hide, I wondered what my parents would think. *"Can't we send you darned kids anywhere without you embarrassing us?"* In that moment, I feared I had permanently soiled the Twomey name.

Then my mind flashed to God. Stealing – even an Oreo cookie – was a sin. I attended Catholic school in my early years and we used to go to confession as an entire class. I imagined myself entering the confessional booth with all my classmates watching, telling the priest of my cookie caper, and then having to kneel for hours as my classmates watched me pump out "Our Father's," "Hail Mary's," and "Glory Be's" as fast as possible so as to not appear to be a mass murderer. I felt lost in a Bermuda Triangle of fear, embarrassment, and shame.

When asked what I was doing, I didn't say anything. I couldn't. If I had opened my mouth, I would have blown chunks of Oreo cookie all over the kitchen.

She sweetly asked me, "Nick, are you hungry? Do you want a cookie?" I sheepishly lied and shook my head "No." Truth be told, I *didn't* want a cookie – I wanted the whole jar, and a big glass of milk to go with it!

While I was as guilty of the proverbial "hand in the cookie jar" as a kid could be (I even broke down in tears out of embarrassment), my hostess was gracious and kind. I don't think she even told my parents. What's more, she gave me another cookie before sending me back to bed.

I suppose all of us have similar stories – things we've said or done that were monumentally embarrassing but rather inconsequential in the big scheme of life.

4

However, we all have stories that cut deeper and consequences that last longer – stories of regret that become defining moments in our lives.

This is my story.

CHAPTER TWO

The VW Van

The year was 1967. The place was St. Clair Shores, Michigan, just outside of Detroit. We were in the thick of the Vietnam War. Racial tensions were high. Burning buildings, lootings, and violent clashes between the police and citizens on the streets of Detroit were occurring only fifteen minutes from our home. Fear had become an unwelcome guest in my nine-year-old world.

One day when I was hanging out with my buddies, my dad asked if we wanted to ride along with him to the store. I loved being in the car with my dad so we all piled into the family Volkswagen van. (Remember those? They were later purchased en masse by the hippy generation and taken by the thousands to Woodstock.)

We pulled into the parking lot of Bill's Market, my favorite store in the whole world. At Bill's Market, you could buy Bazooka bubblegum for a penny, red licorice dollars three for a penny, and wax buckteeth for a nickel.

Rather than inviting my friends and me into the store with him, my dad told us to wait in the car. I suspect he simply didn't want to unleash six nine-year-old boys on an unsuspecting clerk. As we waited in the car, I made my ill-fated attempt at fame.

Irresistible Temptation

While waiting for my dad and talking Detroit Tiger baseball with my buddies, heatedly debating whether Norm Cash or Willie Horton was the better hitter, I noticed that my dad had left the keys in the ignition. I don't know if that was an oversight or if my dad just assumed I wouldn't do anything stupid. If it was the latter, he overestimated me.

There they hung – the car keys – swinging gently back and forth like an apple ready to be plucked. For some unexplainable reason, those keys were luring me, inviting me, calling out to me. No, they were begging me, "Start the engine!"

Somehow I concluded that if I could start the engine, rev the gas a time or two, and then quickly turn it off before my dad returned, I would be elevated to rock star status by my posse of friends. Men started cars and revved engines, and I was determined to do something manly.

It's scary how twisted our minds can be, whether we are nine or forty-nine. In my mind, starting the car created visions of grandeur. I envisioned my feat of bravery and courage being recounted around backyard bonfires. I saw cute little girls at St. Margaret's Catholic school speaking in hushed tones in the hallway: "There's Nick...He started his dad's car!" And they would openly flirt for my attention as I walked by.

Oh yes, starting the engine would change my life. Indeed it did...

Loose Lips

Out of my mouth came defining words that would lead to a defining moment in my life: "I bet I can start the car."

There it was – I had said it. It was out there, my braggadocios claim.

In unison, my friends responded, "No you can't."

There was a lot of octane to their "No," and it was an affront to my nine-year-old manhood. It was game time, and I was determined to show them I had plenty of game. Without hesitation I responded, "Yes I can."

"No...You can't!"

"Yes I can!" After several more volleys along with a few double and triple dog dares, it was time to put up or shut up.

I swaggered from the back to the front of the van with my best "I'm badder than bad" look. I was sure they were all impressed. I was also sure legendary status was but a key-turn away.

Funny thing though. I was swaggering on the outside but staggering on the inside. As I approached the front of the car, those keys that only moments ago had looked so inviting suddenly looked menacing, terrifying, even evil. What would actually happen when I turned the key? I had more questions than answers, but I had painted myself into the proverbial corner.

Choking in the Clutch

To this day I still don't know much about cars – they are largely a mystery to me. I am your basic "fill the tank with gas, change an occasional tire, and top off the essential fluids" kind of guy. Trying to figure out how to change windshield wiper blades can transform me into a raving lunatic.

But at age nine I knew even less. I didn't know that the VW van was a manual transmission. I didn't know what a clutch was. I didn't know that my dad had left the car engaged in reverse. I didn't know how the gears meshed. I didn't know that unless you put your foot on the clutch, the car would lurch backward. In other words, I didn't know what I didn't know.

None of that mattered. Having passed the point of no return, I turned over the ignition while my stomach simultaneously began to turn over. I had a bad feeling…

CHAPTER THREE

Wrecked

We all experience certain feelings – physical feelings, like the flu, or the feeling you get when you mix too much wasabi in with your sushi and it feels like your brain is going to fly out of the top of your skull.

But there are other feelings – *gut feelings* – when you're about to do or say something and a voice in your head screams, "Stop!" As I neared the front of the VW van I heard that voice, but I ignored it. Bad decision.

As I turned over the ignition, I discovered the van had a mind of its own. It lurched violently backward. It lurched so hard I smacked my head on the windshield and received a nice goose egg.

But the dent in my head paled in comparison with the dent in the car behind us. At the precise moment I turned over the ignition, a brand new burgundy '67 Cadillac – all shiny and new – was driving behind our very used and beat up VW van. In the twinkling of an eye, I caved in the entire passenger's side of the Cadillac.

The Gift That Keeps on Giving

I have a few distinct memories about that moment. First, my rock-star status faded like a shooting star. I went from "I'm the baddest nine-year-old around" to crying so hard I was hyperventilating.

Crying like that in front of your friends is not cool. Cool is saying, *I meant to do that 'cause I'm a rebel with a cause.* Uncool is turning purple and crying so hard you're about to vomit.

I also remember feeling overwhelming guilt. Sometimes we feel guilty because other people have projected their expectations on us and we don't live up to them.

We may not actually *be* guilty, mind you. We haven't necessarily broken any legal or moral code. It's just that there are some human beings with Ph.D.'s in what I call "Guiltology" who love to use guilt to manipulate us.

I knew a few nuns in grade school who had fine-tuned guilt into a sort of religion of its own. Sister Robert Marie, my fourth grade teacher, was the patron saint of this order. It was the religion of *"Straighten up or I'll beat you senseless with a ruler and God will breathe hell-fire down on you and you'll be saying Hail Mary's, Our Father's and Glory Be's until your knees bleed!"*

But there's another kind of guilt we all experience that is based on our failures. It is both *objective* (we did something wrong) and *subjective* (we feel bad about it). This kind of guilt is not induced from the outside. It comes from within. Unless you're a full-blooded sociopath, when you mess up, you know it.

The simple truth is that sometimes we feel guilty because we *are* guilty. When you commit adultery, lie, or steal, do you ever feel noble? Do you find yourself anxious to come home and announce to your children, "Hey kids, I cheated on Mom…It was great!"

I didn't think so.

Sometimes when we do wrong we may feel slick or sly or even satisfied, but that feeling never lasts. In the dark of night, lying on your bed, don't expect to feel good. You won't. You will feel crappy. You will feel guilty...because you are. Thankfully, admitting that simple truth is half the solution.

As I rubbed my sore head and surveyed the damage I had caused, I quickly realized, "There's no ducking out of this one. There's no rationalizing, minimizing, or negotiating my way out of this."

I briefly thought of blaming my friends by claiming, "They dared me!" but I knew the old Adam blaming Eve and Eve blaming the serpent trick wouldn't work. I was in up to my neck and I was in it alone. The hard reality was this wasn't my friends' fault. It wasn't my parents' fault. It wasn't society's fault. It was my fault.

Tough Times

What was I supposed to say to my dad? "Sorry"? That seemed pretty lame considering the gravity of what I had done. Even at age nine I knew the financial burden two wrecked cars would put on my dad.

I was one of eight children, raised in a home where hand-me-down socks and shoes were the norm. School shopping was looking at what an older brother or sister had worn the year before. Cars were driven with bald tires, empty gas tanks, and rust holes in the floorboard where you could see the open road below you in the back seat.

On top of all the predictable, normal financial challenges my parents faced, I had incurred a debt I could not possibly repay. *If I was going to live to see another day, it would only be because someone else paid the debt for me.*

When my father came out of the store I wanted to die. I was crushed, embarrassed, and ashamed. But mostly I was deeply sorry I had caused this mess. I was sorry for the owners of the vehicle (who were outside my window threatening me with great bodily harm – people didn't worry about lawsuits in those days), and I was particularly sorry for my wonderful, patient, hardworking dad.

The disappointment in his eyes along with a look that said, "What was I thinking leaving the keys in the car?" caused me pain that was almost unbearable.

My dad was a patient man and not prone to physical punishment (my mom was the designated spanker in the family), but if at that moment he had dragged me out of the car and blistered my little fanny, I would have understood completely. There would have been no cries of protest from me (and there would have been cheers from the other car owner). In a strange sort of way, physical pain would have been a welcome relief from the mental anguish I felt.

The Cry for Justice

I am often intrigued by the human response to things that go awry, the things we consider to be an outrage. Some kid on the school bus gets picked on by a bully and we cry, "That's not fair!"

A cop closes out the bar, drives home drunk, causes an accident and gets away with it, and we cry, "That's not fair."

A married woman with a loving husband who would make fantastic parents cannot get pregnant, while a twenty-two-year-old unwed mother is pregnant for the third time and we say, "That's not fair."

A politician fails to properly file his taxes and ends up as the U.S. Secretary of the Treasury and we say, "What's up with *that*?!"

We all have a sense of fairness, even if we disagree on where to set the bar. But as I look back on that accident, there was nothing fair about it. It wasn't fair what I did to my dad. It wasn't fair what I did to the other car owners. The whole thing stunk of unfairness, and when something is unfair we rise up in moral indignation demanding fairness.

But if all of life was about fairness and justice – getting exactly what we deserve – what would have become of me that day?

Juvenile home for naughty nine-year-olds, with years of forced labor to pay off the debt? That certainly would have been one option.

The Longing for Mercy

The fact that I was able to return home and live another day had nothing to do with justice or fairness. Justice – which is getting exactly what we deserve – is something we find mighty appealing provided we are on the right side of the fence. But given the fact that I had fallen off on the wrong side of the fence I had very little interest in justice. Instead, I had an intense interest in mercy.

Mercy is about *not* getting what you deserve. Mercy is about cutting someone who has failed some slack. If my dad had chosen justice (and it was his to choose), it would have been reasonable and fair. It's what I expected, given the consequences of one stupid, pride-filled act of bravado that caused such a colossal mess.

Defining Moments

Have you ever had a moment like this? Suddenly you are confronted with the inescapable truth of something you've said or done, and as much as you wish you could rewind the tape – take it back and get a "do-over" – you can't.

Maybe there are names and faces flashing through your head, people you've hurt or others who have hurt you.

The temptation is usually to minimize it, rationalize it, or brush it off as no big deal. In other words, "cope." But what if there was something better than merely coping? What if we didn't have to minimize, rationalize, trivialize, or medicate our sorrows and hurts, both ones we've caused and ones we've endured? What if we could get free from our failures and actually grow from them? Would it be worth it to you to finally unlock the ball and chain of regrets and hurts and bitterness from *your* past?

I had no choice but to face the reality of what I had created. There simply wasn't any wiggle room and I wasn't sophisticated enough at age nine to concoct some lame excuse. I was guilty, and that was that.

As I waited for whatever was coming to me, I considered my options. I also started plotting how I could repay the debt. I had $1.70 in spare change in my piggy bank. That was a start. I figured I could collect pop bottles out of ditches and make another $2.00 per week. And then I added up all my other assets. They amounted to zero.

I moved on to another option: I could run away. Lots of people try that. We humans frequently run from our problems and failures to new cities, better jobs, better marriages, etc. Today, I live in a stunningly beautiful part of northwest Michigan with lakes and woods that are so beautiful they entice troubled hearts to move here and start over. The trouble is, they bring their troubled hearts with them.

In any event, the run-away option for nine-year-olds didn't seem very practical even to a nine year old. I didn't want to end up on somebody's milk carton.

Worse yet, I feared being sent to live in the convent with nuns. Being sent to Antarctica to live with the penguins would have been more appealing.

So there I sat, out of options and with no chance of paying back the debt I owed. Despair gripped my frightened heart. What would happen in the next ten minutes would change my life forever.

CHAPTER FOUR

The Golden Arches

Over the next several minutes my dad worked his fatherly magic. He calmed down the owners of the other vehicle, squared away the insurance with the police, and then came back to the van, which was damaged but still drivable.

It has been said that "Silence is golden," but the silence in our van was crushing. We drove home in total silence, with the exception of an occasional whimper that leaked out of me.

When we turned on to Vandover – the street I grew up on – my dad stopped the car and said, "Boys, I think it's time for you to head home." My friends exited the car like prisoners on death row running for freedom. I remember seeing the look in their eyes as we drove away. As one, this look said, "See you at your funeral."

I don't remember much being said after my friends left. There were no lectures of *"What were you thinking?"* There were no scoldings, groundings, spankings, or anything else. In the awkward silence of the van, I had a sense that Dad was deep in thought – almost as though he were up to something.

Then it happened. Rather than stopping at our house, my dad drove on by, turned off our street, and headed back toward Bill's Market. I thought there must be unfinished business at the store, but I was wrong. What happened next could not have been more unexpected.

The Shock of Grace

If *justice* is getting exactly what we deserve and if *mercy* is *not* getting what we deserve, then *grace* (unmerited, unexpected, and undeserved love) is getting what we *don't* deserve.

My dad turned on his blinker (which still worked), and there they were – the Golden Arches. I briefly thought to myself, "Did I die in that accident and go to heaven?"

I couldn't believe what was happening. My dad was turning into a cool new burger joint called McDonald's! Bear in mind that in 1967 there were no Burger Kings, Wendy's, Taco Bells, or Arby's. McDonald's was it, period.

Those golden arches looked like heaven, and in my experience, regular people didn't go to McDonald's. Rich people did, and we were not rich. My blunder had just made us considerably poorer. Inexplicably, my dad had decided to scrounge up the money to take me to McDonald's for lunch.

I knew my dad couldn't afford McDonald's. I knew that our being there meant real sacrifice on his part, making his act of graciousness and generosity as unexplainable as it later became life changing. Silence, fear, and guilt spontaneously turned to joy, gratitude, and relief in that dented, beat-up VW van. To this day, I wonder where dad came up with the money to take me to McDonald's that summer afternoon.

Do the math: I wreck two cars and cause a lot of grief. In exchange I end up with a cheeseburger, fries, and a Coke. Go figure. It may not seem like a big deal to you, but it had a profound impact on me six years later.

Looking back, I know my dad saw how broken I was over what I had done. He knew my tears were more than sorrow for the trouble I was in. My tears were more about the sorrow I was causing him.

How would my dad have responded had I attempted to defend my actions and "explain myself?" I'll never know for sure, but I have a pretty clear idea it would have been a bad idea. I've learned the hard way that defending yourself when you are so patently guilty is just plain stupid. Take your lumps and move on...

In this case, however, all the lumps I took were self-inflicted. I was beating myself up so bad that if my soul had been x-rayed, it would have looked like Rocky at the end of, well, at the end of every single *Rocky* movie!

Graciously, my dad decided not to "pile on" (to use a football metaphor). As I sat in my wrecked state, my dad did something extraordinary: rather than leaving me to swim in an ocean of guilt and remorse, he threw me a life-line in the form of a burger, fries, and Coke. It was his way of saying, "Nick, I love you. You mean more to me than anything in the world. You mean more to me than our van, and more to me than a brand new Cadillac, and more to me than the money it will cost to fix them."

Connecting the Dots

Fast forward six years. I was fifteen years old and on the outside I had a lot going for me – I was a good athlete, popular in school, etc. But on the inside I had this deep sense that something was missing.

Toward the end of my sophomore year in high school a guy from my school came to my home to talk with me about God. His name was Kevin Gephart. Kevin was a church kid raised with the Bible. He read it, understood it, and his life was shaped by it. I was a church kid too, but I had never read the Bible. Truth be told, I was afraid of the Bible and most other things related to church.

Kevin explained to me who Jesus was. I knew Jesus was the central figure of

Christmas and Easter, but beyond that I had no idea who he was or *why* he came. No one had ever explained that to me. I thought he was a holier version of Santa Claus and the Easter Bunny, or perhaps the church's version of a super-hero.

Kevin, on the other hand, seemed to have a clear sense of just who Jesus was and why he came. He explained that Jesus wasn't just a good teacher, a man of compassion, a spiritual guide, though he was certainly those things. He told me that Jesus was God, as in *the* God who created the whole world.

He went on to tell me that Jesus took on human flesh – became one of us – because he loved us and wanted to have a personal relationship with us. That was mind-blowing to me. Why would he want anything to do with me? If he was really God, he knew what a mess I was.

Nonetheless, Kevin explained that Jesus loved me unconditionally, with no strings attached. Not an "I'll love you if…" sort of love but a flat-out complete love – just the way I was – and that he came to earth to rescue me and the rest of the human race from the mess of sin *we* caused. Kevin explained that Jesus came to *"pay a debt he did not owe on behalf of all the guilty who owed a debt we could not repay."*

Bingo. I understood. I flashed back to the day I had wrecked two cars and received McDonald's in exchange. Suddenly the dots connected. Suddenly the message of grace – of getting what I didn't deserve – all made sense. What my dad did for me on the day I wrecked the car is what Jesus did for me on the cross.

And he's still doing it. For all of us who've wrecked things or hurt people because of our over-inflated view of ourselves, God, our heavenly father, looks at us in our brokenness and shame and says "Son/daughter, I forgive you. I love you – no strings attached. I've already paid your debt. If you'll let me, I'd love to take you through the golden arches – burger, fries, and Coke on me."

In most areas of life my dad was a simple, uncomplicated man. But on the day I wrecked the family car, he was a giant, a theologian, even a savior of sorts. At a time in my life when I had given up on God, I was able to look back at the car wreck and say, "If God treats me like my dad treated me, I'm in."

Thanks, Dad. That one life lesson not only changed my life but it sent me on a lifelong adventure of helping others experience the transforming power of grace. I can't wait to see you again under the big golden arches in heaven.

NICK TWOMEY, founding paster of Bay Pointe Community Church in Traverse City, Michigan is passionate about building relational bridges that connect people in authentic ways – especially ways that connect people to God. To learn more visit *www.nicktwomey.com.*